This Walker book belongs to:

For Pixie

First published 2017 by Walker Books Ltd,
87 Vauxhall Walk, London SE11 5HJ

This edition published 2019

2 4 6 8 10 9 7 5 3 1

This book has been typeset in Trixie

Printed in China

British Library Cataloguing in Publication Data:
a catalogue record for this book is available from the British Library

ISBN 978-1-4063-7829-0

www.walker.co.uk

COUNTING WITH TINY CAT

Viviane Schwarz

NONE

ONE

TWO

THREE

FOUR

MORE

EVEN MORE

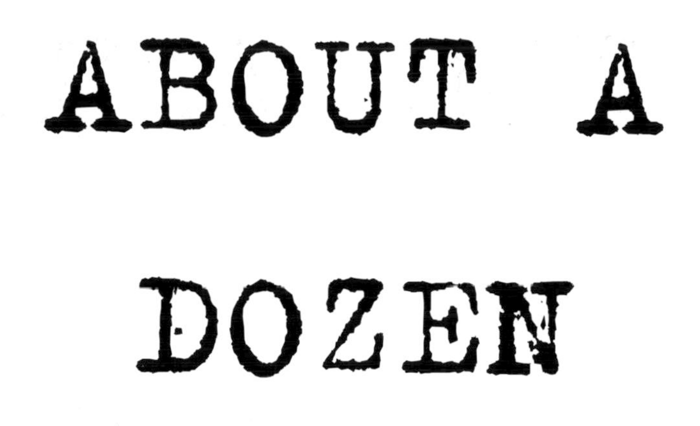
ABOUT A
DOZEN

LOTS

AS

MANY

AS

YOU

CAN

GET

SOME EXTRA

TOO MANY

ENOUGH

Look out for:

"Witty, original and charming ...
extremely successful with toddlers"
The Sunday Times

A *Publishers Weekly*
Best Book of the Year

978-1-4063-2499-0

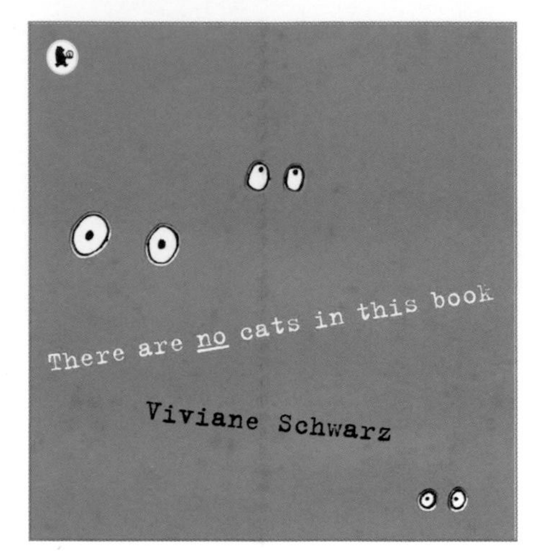

"A clever, interactive read"
Herald

Shortlisted for the
Kate Greenaway Medal

978-1-4063-3102-8

Winner of the Children's Book Award

"A hilarious romp"
The New York Times

978-1-4063-6090-5